Charlie Claus

Santa's Best Friend

by Nina Pellegrini

DERRYDALE BOOKS
New York • Avenel, New Jersey

To
Charlie
love
Santa

Charlie Claus is Santa's best friend. And although you may never have heard of him, he is very important to Santa.

Charlie takes his job as Santa's best friend very seriously.

Every night at nine o'clock when Santa goes to sleep, Charlie curls up at the end of the bed to warm Santa's feet.

Every morning at seven
o'clock when Santa wakes
up, Charlie brings him his
bathrobe and slippers, so he
won't be cold.

Every day at twelve o'clock, he sits with Santa and keeps him company while they have lunch.

And every afternoon Charlie trots beside Santa
playing and doing tricks, and Santa roars
with laughter,
"Ho, Ho, Ho!"

Last Christmas there
were more children than ever.
Every day the mail
brought Santa

more and more letters from boys and girls asking for toys.

There were rag dolls and teddy bears to sew, paper kites to string, doll houses to build, and airplanes, boats, and fire engines to paint.

As Santa and his elves worked harder and harder, Charlie began to worry about Santa more and more.

Every night at nine o'clock, Charlie curled up at the end of Santa's bed, but Santa didn't crawl into bed until very late, and by then he was too sleepy to notice if his feet were cold.

Every morning at seven o'clock,
Charlie brought Santa his bathrobe
and slippers, but Santa hurried to
work so fast that he forgot to put
them on.

Every day at twelve o'clock, Charlie sat at the table by himself waiting for Santa to come, but Santa was too busy to eat.

And every afternoon Charlie ran beside Santa,
doing tricks, but Santa never noticed. He was
too busy working.

Santa was looking very tired. He
was sneezing a lot. He was losing some of
his rolypoly belly from skipping meals.
And he had stopped laughing.
"What if Santa gets sick?" thought
Charlie. "That will be terrible!

Who will deliver the toys to all the children?"

If only there was something he could do to help!
Charlie had never been
very good with his paws,
but he decided to
give it a try.

But no matter what Charlie tried to do, he made more and more of a mess.

The elves began to giggle,
but Charlie didn't give up.

BEAR STUFFING

Charlie was being more trouble than help, until finally Santa said, "Please just sit quietly and watch."

So Charlie sat quietly next to a big can of red paint. When Santa walked by, Charlie stood up and his tail landed wham! right in the paint can. "Ho, ho, ho,"

laughed Santa.

Charlie wagged his tail harder and harder. "Ho, ho, ho," Santa laughed. "At last you have found a job you can do."

Charlie looked behind him. His bright red tail was swishing red paint onto the fire engine.

Charlie howled with joy.
"Aaoooooh, Aaoooooh, Aaoooooh."
"Ho Ho Ho," laughed Santa.
"Aaoooooh, Aaoooooh,"
howled Charlie.

Charlie had finally found a way to help Santa.
Santa put him in charge of all the painting. Charlie
painted doll houses, airplanes,
boats, and fire engines, and

the smiles on the faces of the rag dolls. This made less work for Santa and the elves.

Soon Santa was feeling like his old self again. He and
Charlie loaded up his sleigh with all the toys that Charlie
had painted.

On Christmas Eve, Santa took to the sky with his best
friend Charlie Claus right beside him.